You're a Star SNOOPY!

Peanuts® characters created
and drawn by Charles M. Schulz

Text by Linda Williams Aber
Background illustrations by Art and Kim Ellis

A GOLDEN BOOK • NEW YORK
Western Publishing Company, Inc., Racine, Wisconsin 53404

Copyright © 1990 United Feature Syndicate, Inc. All rights reserved. Printed in the U.S.A. No part of this book may be reproduced or copied in any form without written permission from the publisher. GOLDEN, GOLDEN & DESIGN, GOLDENCRAFT, A GOLDEN LOOK-LOOK BOOK, and A GOLDEN LOOK-LOOK BOOK & DESIGN are trademarks of Western Publishing Company, Inc. Library of Congress Catalog Card Number: 88-81452 ISBN: 0-307-11728-6/ISBN: 0-307-61728-9 (lib bdg.)
B C D E F G H I J K L M

"Yecchh! I feel terrible," Snoopy said, holding his stomach. "I should never have eaten that last box of Ace Chocolate Chip Cookies. Contest or no contest, not even a trip to Hollywood is worth feeling this sick."

In the past three weeks Snoopy had eaten twenty-five boxes of cookies. He tore off the box tops and sent them to the Ace Chocolate Chip Cookie Company. Every box top he sent in gave him another chance to win a free trip for two to Hollywood. The winner would also get to try out for a part in a big Hollywood movie.

"It's my chance to be a real star," Snoopy said to himself. He thought it would be a good idea to take a walk, but he was too full to move. Snoopy decided to lie down and wait to hear from the cookie company.

"When they see twenty-five box tops from the same address, they're sure to know that I'm their guy," he thought.

The next day, however, Snoopy began to think that maybe twenty-five box tops wasn't enough. Before he could even think about eating another box of cookies, Charlie Brown came running over. He was holding a letter.

"It's here," Charlie Brown shouted. "Snoopy, you got a letter from the Ace Chocolate Chip Cookie Company!"

Snoopy read the letter very carefully. After he finished
reading, he just stared at the paper in silence for a minute.

Suddenly Snoopy jumped up and started dancing for joy. Charlie Brown realized what had happened and he joined in and shouted, "Snoopy won the contest. He's going to Hollywood!"

The next thing Snoopy did was call his friend Woodstock to tell him the good news. "It will be good to have a friend around when I become a big Hollywood star," he thought to himself. "I'm going to Hollywood, and you're coming with me!" Snoopy told Woodstock.

Woodstock was as happy as he could be. The news made everyone do the same happy dance.

Getting ready for a trip to Hollywood was not easy. "If I'm going to be a star," thought Snoopy, "I have to look like a star. Sunglasses will complete the look!"

Snoopy tried on every pair of sunglasses he had, until he found just the right one. "No one will ever recognize me in these," he said with a laugh.

"Hi, Snoopy," said Linus as he walked past the future Hollywood star.
"Good grief!" thought Snoopy.

At last the time came for Snoopy and Woodstock to leave
for Hollywood. Their friends gathered to say good-bye.
  "Have a great trip, Snoopy, old boy," said Charlie Brown.
  "If you need any advice, just call me," said Lucy.

"We'll miss you," said Linus.

"WAAHHH!" cried Sally.

"Parting is such sweet sorrow," thought Snoopy dramatically.

Snoopy and Woodstock boarded a jet plane headed for
Hollywood. After takeoff Snoopy turned to his friend and
said, "Woodstock, you are now sitting next to the future
award-winning star of the silver screen. Don't worry, little
friend. I'll always have time for you."

Several hours later Snoopy looked out the window. Down
on the ground he saw what he'd been waiting for the whole
flight. It was the famous Hollywood sign.

"We're here, Woodstock!" Snoopy shouted. "Tinseltown!
Home of the stars. Hollywood!"

Snoopy and Woodstock spent that day and the next sightseeing. They visited the famous Sidewalk of the Stars.

"What do you think, Woodstock? It looks like there's plenty of room on this sidewalk for two more stars, one for you and one for me. I want mine right next to Lassie's. I'll have to speak to the studio about that when we get there," Snoopy said.

"We're late," exclaimed Snoopy when he realized what time it was. "We're supposed to be at the movie studio right now."

When Snoopy and Woodstock met the famous film
director Cecil B. De Dog, Snoopy got an unpleasant surprise.
The director paid no attention to Snoopy at all. Instead, he
invited Woodstock into his office. "The guy never even
shook my paw," Snoopy said to himself.

Snoopy could hear the director talking to Woodstock. He
didn't like what he was hearing at all. De Dog told Woodstock
that he had the makings of a big star.

"I'm supposed to be the big star. I'm the one who ate all
those cookies," Snoopy moaned.

Then Snoopy heard the director say that Woodstock would be perfect for the lead role in his next picture, *Trick or Tweet*. The director rushed Woodstock out of his office and onto the movie set.

Two days passed and Woodstock was so busy that Snoopy didn't even get to see him. "I'm miserable," Snoopy thought. "We came all the way to Hollywood so I could be a star. Now Woodstock is too busy even to talk to me. In fact, I can't even get near him anymore."

Suddenly Snoopy had a great idea. "Hollywood stars love publicity," he thought. "I'll pretend that I'm a newspaper reporter and set up an interview with Woodstock."

When Snoopy arrived for the interview, Woodstock looked tired and unhappy. Snoopy started asking questions for his newspaper story. Woodstock said that being a movie star was exciting, but it was also very hard work. Woodstock said he didn't like having to wake up early for rehearsals each day. Even though the movie studio had built a special dressing room nest for him, Woodstock said he missed his nest and friends at home. His biggest complaint was that being a movie star kept him from seeing his good friend Snoopy.

Snoopy couldn't stand it anymore. He took off his
reporter outfit and let Woodstock see who he really was.
Woodstock was very happy to see his friend.

"Start packing, Woodstock," said Snoopy. "We're going
home." Woodstock told the movie director he wanted to go
home. Cecil B. De Dog said he understood and that he would
get another actor to take Woodstock's place.

Then Snoopy picked up Woodstock, nest and all, and
headed for home.

When the two friends got there, it was even better than they had remembered it. Everyone was very glad to see them. With no movie rehearsals to get up for, Woodstock could sleep as long as he wanted to.

Charlie Brown was so happy to see Snoopy that he brought him all his meals early.

Lucy didn't even get mad when Snoopy kissed her on the nose.

As Charlie Brown hugged his friend, Snoopy thought happily, "Fame and fortune aren't everything. I get the best star treatment right here at home!"